Babe Ruth
and the
Home Run Derby

★★★★★★

OTHER YEARLING BOOKS YOU WILL ENJOY:

THE TERRIBLE TICKLER (ALL-STAR MEATBALLS #2),
Stephen Mooser
AGGRO MOVES (STREET WIZARDS #1), Troy Bannon
DUMP DAYS, Jerry Spinelli
TWELVE-YEAR-OLD VOWS REVENGE!, Stephen Roos
MY SECRET ADMIRER, Stephen Roos
MY HORRIBLE SECRET, Stephen Roos
THE TERRIBLE TRUTH, Stephen Roos
CHOCOLATE FEVER, Robert Kimmel Smith
JELLY BELLY, Robert Kimmel Smith
BOBBY BASEBALL, Robert Kimmel Smith

YEARLING BOOKS/YOUNG YEARLINGS/YEARLING CLASSICS are designed especially to entertain and enlighten young people. Patricia Reilly Giff, consultant to this series, received her bachelor's degree from Marymount College and a master's degree in history from St. John's University. She holds a Professional Diploma in Reading and a Doctorate of Humane Letters from Hofstra University. She was a teacher and reading consultant for many years, and is the author of numerous books for young readers.

For a complete listing of all Yearling titles,
write to
Dell Readers Service,
P.O. Box 1045,
South Holland, IL 60473.

Babe Ruth and the Home Run Derby

★ ★ ★ ★ ★ ★

STEPHEN MOOSER

Illustrated by
GEORGE ULRICH

A YEARLING BOOK

Published by
Dell Publishing
a division of
Bantam Doubleday Dell Publishing Group, Inc.
666 Fifth Avenue
New York, New York 10103

ISBN: 0-440-40486-X

Printed in the United States of America

September 1992

10 9 8 7 6 5 4 3 2 1

OPM

LIST OF CHARACTERS

They're hilarious, they're strange, and even though they're not jocks, they are into sports. . . . Here's the All-Star Meatballs starting line-up.

HOMER KING: He's been seen at Bayview School in his pajama top and also in his underwear, but he's best known for his skill at hitting home runs and throwing meatballs.

MOLLY JAMES: She's got a bow in her hair the size of a TV antenna and a dog under her desk named Godzilla that only she can see.

DARRYL PUMPWATER: He's got the whole Meatballs Club groaning, but not because his clothes are on inside out and backward. It's because no one can bear his corny jokes.

KATE BARNETT: She can see things better than anyone, even though she's blind.

NICOLE MARTIN: She can dance, play football, and roller skate too. She's easy to spot: There's a ponytail shooting from the top of her head like a hairy fountain.

LUIS CRUZON: He can walk across a tightrope, juggle a fishbowl, and balance a birthday cake on his head. Pretty special tricks, especially for a boy with only one arm.

And let's not forget . . .

MR. FOSTER: Before he became the Meatballs' teacher he was a monkey trainer in the circus. He believes that students, like monkeys, learn best when a banana is the reward. A bunch hangs above his desk.

MAXIE BUTTS: He's big, mean, and full of nasty tricks. He and his gang, the Jokers, don't get along with the Meatballs. Not one bit.

For Mrs. Hawn,
Mrs. McCullough,
and all their students at the
Crossroads School, Paoli, Pennsylvania

CONTENTS

CHAPTER 1

Food Fight

IT WAS the first day of school. The Bayview cafeteria was filled with the smell of meatballs and the rattling of trays. Everyone was talking at once. Everyone but a sad-eyed boy with wavy red hair who was looking for a place to sit. His name was Homer King. And he was new.

I wish I had a friend, he thought. His brown pants were as rumpled as an old paper bag. Mismatched yellow and green socks flopped limply over his black shoes.

1

He looked across the crowded room and sighed. His last school had been horrible. He hadn't had a single friend. No one had asked him to be in any clubs.

There was an empty spot at a nearby table. He sighed again, shuffled over, and put down his plate of meatballs and his bowl of soup.

I hope this place is better than the last, he thought, sliding onto the bench.

There were six other people at the table. Across the way was a girl with a giant bow in her hair the size of a TV antenna. Next to her was a boy in an inside-out shirt and baseball cap. Next to him a girl with a single ponytail sprouting from the top of her head.

"Hi," said Homer, in a bare whisper.

Whap! Someone slapped his back. Hard.

"Ow!" said Homer. He turned around. Standing behind him was a tall boy in a floppy blue cap and suspenders.

"Say hello to Maxie Butts!" said the boy, grinning.

"Hello," said Homer softly.

"Say, aren't you kind of little for a base-ball star?" said the boy. He was missing most of his front teeth. Every s he said came out as a hiss.

Homer blinked his big brown eyes. "Are you talking to me?"

"Make like a camper, Butts. Take a hike!" snapped the girl in the big bow. "Leave him alone. Can't you see he's eating?"

Homer turned to the girl and smiled. She had round red cheeks and pretty blue eyes. He'd seen her earlier that morning. Like everyone else at the table, she was in his new class.

"Keep out of this, Molly," growled Maxie. "I'm not talking to you. I'm talking to the squirt here." He slapped Homer again on the back. "Aren't I, kid?"

Homer gulped. He didn't know what to say. All he could do was what he always did when he was nervous. He dug into his pocket and pulled out a broken black comb. Then he began combing his hair and humming.

"You may be a homer king but you're not going to beat me in the derby," said Maxie. He jerked his thumb in the direction of the next table. It was filled with sour-faced boys in black T-shirts. "The Jokers and I intend to keep that trophy."

The boys at the next table made ugly faces and tried to look tough. One of them stabbed a meatball with his fork, then shook it at Homer.

"I think you made a mistake," said Homer in a squeaky little voice. He shook his head. "I don't even play baseball."

"Oh, sure. Then how come they call you Homer King, huh?" Maxie gave Homer a goofy look. "Do you think I'm dumb or something?"

"No one thinks that," said Molly. "You're smart, Maxie. Smarter than most."

"Really?"

"Sure. Smarter than most . . . potatoes," said Molly.

Maxie gasped. "Take that back! I'm not smarter than most potatoes." He patted his chest. "I'm smarter than ALL potatoes."

Everyone laughed. Maxie scratched his head and tried to figure out what was so funny.

"The Jokers better watch out," said Molly. She pointed at Homer. "This guy is a champ. He's going to win that trophy for us on Friday. Easy."

"Huh? I am?" said Homer.

"Yep!" said Molly. She grinned. "This table is about to become full of Home Run Derby kings." She gave Homer a giant wink. "Maxie is right. Anyone nicknamed Homer King has got to be a superstar."

"Me? Superstar?" said Homer, grinning. Then, suddenly, he wrinkled his face. "Wait a minute. What's a home run derby?"

"It's a contest we have at Bayview every year," said the boy in the inside-out clothes. From class Homer remembered his name was Darryl Pumpwater. "Every-

5

body gets three pitches. The person that hits the ball the farthest is the champ of the whole school."

"And that's going to be me," said Maxie. He gave Homer's shoulder a hard squeeze. "If you know what's good for you, squirt, you'll drop out. Now. Before it's too late."

"Drop out? But I haven't even entered," said Homer.

"Don't worry. I'll sign you up," said Molly. She raised her chin. "It's about time this school had a new derby king. Someone who isn't a bully or a bigmouth."

"But . . ." said Homer. He looked around the table desperately. Everyone was making a terrible mistake. Homer King wasn't his nickname. It was his real name. And he didn't know a thing about baseball. "Maybe I shouldn't enter," he said. "Since I'm new, maybe—"

"Don't even think about it," said Molly, cutting him off. She pointed at the Jokers. "Those guys may be tough. And mean. And the bullies of the school. But they don't scare us! Not one bit!"

Homer gave the Jokers a little wave. The Jokers looked back and snarled. Homer moaned and began combing his hair.

"Just wait till Friday, big shot," said Maxie.

Homer gulped, then combed faster.

"I can hardly wait for the derby," said Molly. She reached out and squeezed Homer's muscle. "Ooooh. You're strong as Superman."

Homer blushed. "Well . . ."

Molly squeezed again. "With muscles like this I bet you could hit a baseball to the moon."

"Well . . ." said Homer.

Molly tapped Homer on the nose. "On Friday you'll be the hero of the school."

"He'll be a soo-per star!" said Nicole Martin. She was the girl with the ponytail atop her head. She reached up and waved it at Homer.

Homer shook his head with wonder. Hero! He couldn't believe it. No one had even liked him at his old school. Here, he was already a hero.

"Tell him," said Molly. "Tell him how you got your famous nickname."

Homer didn't know what to say. He'd never been called a hero and a superstar before. If he told the truth it would ruin everything. Before he knew what he was doing he'd picked up a gooey meatball and was showing it around.

"See this baseball?" he said, making things up as he went along. "I got the name Homer King because I hit balls like this over the fence!" Homer looked at Molly and smiled. She smiled back. She was so pretty!

"Pow!" said Homer in his squeaky voice. "I hit 'em all the time."

Everyone clapped.

Homer grinned.

"Ah, go on," said Maxie. He flicked the back of Homer's head. "You're no home run hitter. You're a meatball, just like that mess in your hands."

"He is not!" said Molly. "Go on, Homer, show him."

"Be a soo-perstar," said Nicole. She

8

grabbed her fountain of hair and pointed it at Maxie. "Show that bully."

Homer shrugged his shoulders and stood up. He held the meatball under Maxie's nose. "They call me Homer King because I hit these a mile. And I can throw them into forever."

"Ah, go on," said Maxie.

"Show him," said Molly.

Homer stepped back to the wall. He drew back his arm. "Watch. I'll throw it over the fence!"

Homer had forgotten he was in the cafeteria. There wasn't any fence. Or any baseball. Only a meatball.

"Whee!" he said, letting it go.

"Hey! Watch where—!" screamed Maxie as the meatball sped his way. He tried to duck, but too late.

KER-SPLAT! The gooey lump of meat slammed into his nose, and stuck!

"Eeee-yew!" said Nicole.

"Whoopsie," said Homer. He put his hands on his cheeks and giggled.

With a meatball for a nose Maxie looked like a circus clown.

"Why you . . . you!" he stammered. He drew back his fist.

"No, no," squeaked Homer.

GRUNCH! A meatball to the mouth cut him off in midsentence. Another Joker, Billy Tubbs, had thrown it.

"Great shot, Billy!" yelled the Jokers. They laughed and slapped each other's hands.

While the Jokers were celebrating, Molly picked up a meatball and threw it at Billy.

"Take that!" she screamed, letting it go.

The meatball landed in a bowl of soup. KER-SPLASH! Everyone got soaked.

"Eeee-yew!" said Nicole.

"Food fight!" yelled Maxie. He plucked the meatball from his nose. Then he ran back to his table and organized his troops. "Battle stations!" he cried.

"Food fight!" yelled Molly.

She put a meatball on her spoon and pulled it back.

"Bombs away!" she shouted, sending the mush missile flying.

Suddenly everyone was running, yelling, and laughing. Milk spilled. Plates clattered to the ground. Some people went down on the slippery floor. Ker-thuck!

Meatballs slammed into faces and arms and backs. Kersplat! Ker-unch! Ker-blam!

Ker-splash! Some of the Jokers were throwing soup.

Th-wock! A meatball squished into Molly's shoulder.

Splat! Another one caught a Joker in the back of the head.

"Food fight!" everyone screamed.

"Meatball 'em!" cried Molly.

"Soup 'em!" said Billy Tubbs.

The cafeteria went crazy. Everyone jumped up to see the show. Some people stood on the benches. Way in the back a kindergartner climbed onto his table.

Splash! He stepped into a bowl of soup, slipped, and went down on his bottom into a plate of meatballs.

"Eeee-yew!" screamed his friends.

Tha-wock! Ker-splat! Ker-plop!

It wasn't a food fight anymore. It was a food war.

Yells, shouts, cheers, and meatballs went bouncing off the cafeteria walls. Then, suddenly, one scream rose above the rest.

"Eeee-yahhh!"

Everyone stopped dead. They recognized the voice. It belonged to the cook, Mrs. Looper. She was running out from behind the counter, waving her arms and yelling like a cavalry charge.

"Eeee-yahhh!"

KER-SPLAT! The last meatball of the war caught her in the back of the neck.

"Whoops!" everyone said at once. Slow as slime the meatball slid down the back of her new white uniform.

Mrs. Looper screeched to a halt. Her face was as red as spaghetti sauce. Her eyes looked ready to explode.

Mrs. Looper cast an angry eye across the room. Everyone had frozen where they stood. At last her eyes settled on Homer

13

and Maxie and all their friends. They were plastered with pieces of meatballs and dripping with soup.

"You, you, you, you, you, and you!" she said, pointing to them all. "Outside!"

"He started it," whined Maxie, pointing to Homer. "Kick that troublemaker out of school."

Mrs. Looper tapped her big foot and glared at Homer. She looked as if she thought Maxie's suggestion might be a good idea.

"I'm a goner," moaned Homer. "A meatball just turned my first day of school into my last."

CHAPTER 2

Wet and Wild

MRS. LOOPER marched everyone out of the cafeteria, down the hall, and outside into the hot sun. Half the people in the small, sad parade had been sitting at the table with Homer. The rest were Jokers.

Maxie came up and jammed Homer in the back with his thumb. "If I get in trouble you'll be real sorry," he whispered. "The principal and I are pals. I can get you kicked out of school. Easy."

"You try that and Godzilla will bite your leg off," said Molly.

Homer gulped and looked quickly about. "Godzilla?" he said.

"Shhhh! No talking!" said Mrs. Looper sharply. She pointed to the bleachers at the edge of the baseball field. "Sit!"

Homer's table sat on one end, the Jokers at the other.

"I won't have food fights in my cafeteria," said Mrs. Looper. She waved her spoon. "If this happens again you'll be kicked out of school. Now, who started this?"

"The squirt!" said Maxie, hissing out the *s*. "The new kid started slinging stuff first."

Mrs. Looper gave Homer a long hard look.

Homer nervously combed his goopy hair and forced a smile. More than anything he didn't want to be kicked out of school. His old school had been horrible. He didn't want to have to go back.

"It was an accident," said Molly. She

16

curled her hands into pretend binoculars. Then focused them on Mrs. Looper. "He didn't mean to throw it."

"I couldn't help it," said Homer in his squeaky little voice. "The meatball slipped."

"The meatball slipped," said Nicole.

"Yes," said Darryl. "The meatball—"

"Meatballs! Meatballs! Meatballs!" shouted Mrs. Looper. "I don't want to hear anything more about meatballs, especially from you—you meatballs!"

"Meatballs?" said Molly.

"Yes, meatballs," said Mrs. Looper. "Molly, that's exactly how you and your friends acted today."

"Sorry," said everyone.

"I'm sorry too," said Mrs. Looper. "But I won't have any more food fights in my cafeteria. From now on Molly's table will eat outside here on the bleachers."

"What about the Jokers?" said Molly. "They were throwing food too."

"You admitted you started it," said Mrs. Looper.

"We have to eat out here every day?" asked Nicole.

"Every day," said Mrs. Looper. "Unless it rains."

Homer looked up at the sky. He wished it were raining right then. The sun was hot. And he was thirsty.

"Mrs. Looper, can I get a drink?" he asked, raising his hand.

Mrs. Looper glanced up at the sun and sighed. "Get a drink from the hose," she said. She pointed to a pair of pipes and some long hoses. "Make it fast."

Homer leapt up and dashed over to the pipes. He picked up one of the hoses. Then he turned on the faucet on one of the pipes.

Back at the bleachers Maxie was teasing the Meatballs.

"Meatballs, man, what a bunch of losers," he said. "Nah, nah, nah, nah, nah —HEY!"

KER-POW! A fat stream of water came shooting up from under the bleachers. Accidentally, Homer had turned on the wrong faucet.

BLAM! the blast from the sprinkler nearly lifted Maxie off the bench.

"Help!" he shouted.

"What are you doing over there?" shouted Mrs. Looper, pointing a shaking finger.

"Sorry. Accident," said Homer. He fumbled to turn off the water. But in his hurry he turned it the wrong way. It shot up higher than ever.

SWOOSH! The water gushed up, soaking Maxie to the skin. For a moment he stood frozen beneath the shower, fuming and dripping. Then he sloshed out of the stands and headed for Homer, his eyes ablaze.

"You're done for!" he said, shaking his fist.

"Who? Me?" said Homer. His hand was still on the faucet.

"Yes, you!" said Maxie. He lowered his head and charged. "You're going to get it now!"

19

Homer didn't wait to see what he was going to get. He ran.

"Help!" he yelled. Without looking back he dashed into the school and sprinted down the hallway.

"Come back here, squirt!" yelled Maxie, shaking his fist.

Homer's arms were pumping. His legs were churning. He skidded around a corner and leapt into the safety of his classroom.

His new teacher, Mr. Foster, was seated on the edge of his desk.

"Hi, Homer," he said. "Did you find the lunch all right?"

Homer looked down at the food on his clothes. "Nope. But the lunch found me."

CHAPTER 3

Godzilla

MR. FOSTER had a warm smile and a bushy mustache. A bunch of bananas hung on a hook above his desk. Before coming to Bayview School, Mr. Foster had taught tricks to monkeys at the Big Top circus. He still believed that everyone worked harder when they were rewarded with bananas.

Maxie stuck his water-soaked head in the door. He looked at Mr. Foster, then at

Homer. "See you at the derby, squirt. Better not chicken out."

"I won't," said Homer in his squeaky little voice.

Maxie waved his fist. Then he disappeared into the hall.

"So you're entering the derby," said Mr. Foster. He put a hand on Homer's shoulder. "I would think someone with a name like yours can hit a ball a mile."

"Lots of people think that," said Homer. He looked up and saw Molly coming through the door. "But, really, I'm not that good."

"Nonsense," said Mr. Foster. He picked a banana from the bunch hanging above his desk. "I'll tell you what. Win the derby and I'll give you this."

Homer rolled his eyes. Mr. Foster must have thought he was still teaching monkeys.

"I hope that bully didn't hurt you," said Molly, hurrying Homer's way. "He's mean to everyone."

Homer took out his comb. Could it be?

Did Molly really care for him? Maybe she thought he was a baseball star. Or maybe she just wanted the trophy for the room. He gave her a big smile and combed his hair.

Together they walked to their desks. "Welcome to the Meatballs Club," said Molly.

"Meatballs Club?" said Homer. "What's that?"

"It's all the kids who fought the Jokers," said Molly. "You and me and Darryl and Nicole. Everyone. We made up the club just now, after Maxie chased you away."

"Really?" said Homer. "I'm in a real club?"

"Yep," said Molly. "Nicole is going to be the president. Our clubhouse will be under the bleachers. That way the Meatballs get to meet every day, at lunch."

Homer giggled. "Meatballs. That's a funny name."

"I think it's neat," said Molly.

"Oh, me too," said Homer quickly. He didn't want to disagree. Even though he'd never been in a club before, he knew the number-one rule: Club members had to stick together.

"Listen, don't worry about Maxie," said Molly, sitting down at the desk across from Homer. "Next time he goes after you, I'll get Godzilla to protect you."

"Godzilla!" said Homer. This was the second time Molly had mentioned that name. "The—the fire-breathing dragon from the movies?"

Molly laughed. "No, silly. My dog. He's a little white poodle." She reached under her desk and patted the air. "He goes everywhere with me."

Homer squinted and looked under Molly's desk. But there wasn't a thing there.

"Godzilla is my kind of dog," said Homer.

And he meant it. Homer was allergic to dogs and cats. Molly's dog was the first one he'd ever met that didn't make his eyes water, his nose run, and the rest of him shake and shiver.

"Go on," said Molly. "Pet him. He won't bite."

"Okay," said Homer. He reached under Molly's desk and petted the air. He felt silly. But he didn't want to hurt Molly's feelings. "Nice doggie. Good Godzilla."

"He's my best friend," said Molly. "Doesn't he have the softest fur?"

Homer petted the air some more and looked dreamily into Molly's face. She was so pretty, even with gobs of spaghetti sauce in her hair. The food fight had turned out to be the best thing that had ever happened. Now he and Molly were both Meatballs. They'd get to eat together for the rest of the year.

Then, suddenly, a terrible thought crossed his mind. He'd forgotten something: the Home Run Derby.

He stared down at his floppy socks. *What's going to happen when everyone finds out I can't hit? Are they still going to want me in their club?*

Homer moaned. He was afraid he already knew the answer.

CHAPTER 4

A Reward

AFTER school Mr. Foster called Homer to his desk.

"I have something for you," said the teacher. He reached up and plucked a banana from the bunch hanging over his desk. "You did very well in class your first day. Here's a banana."

Homer looked at the banana. He felt a little like one of Mr. Foster's last students, the monkeys. But he felt kind of special too. The banana was the first thing he'd ever been awarded. Ever. In his whole life.

"Keep it up and there will be many more to come," said Mr. Foster. He opened the top drawer of his desk. "And I have something else for you too."

"Really?" said Homer. "For me?"

Mr. Foster pulled out an old red T-shirt. A big number three was on the front. RUTH was written on the back.

"This once belonged to a great hitter," said Mr. Foster. "I'm going to let you borrow it. Wear it at the derby. You'll hit a homer for sure."

"I will?" said Homer.

"You can't miss," said Mr. Foster. "It's a lucky T-shirt."

"I'll need more than luck," said Homer. He shook his head. "I'm not that good."

Mr. Foster scowled. "You have to believe in yourself. Don't you want to win more bananas?"

Homer nodded. Getting a prize was fun. All at once he knew why monkeys learned so fast. They liked getting prizes too. No wonder Mr. Foster was such a good teacher.

Homer clutched the banana tight. "I'll try my best. I promise."

"I knew you'd say that," said Mr. Foster.

CHAPTER 5

The Babe's Shirt

THE NEXT day Homer wore his lucky red T-shirt to school, under his jacket.

When he got to class Molly was already in her seat. There was a silver whistle around her neck, and another TV-antenna-sized bow in her hair. She made binoculars with her hands and watched him walk her way.

"Hi!" she said, as he swung into his seat.

"Hi," said Homer. He smiled, but

couldn't think of anything else to say. He took out his comb and began to work on his hair.

"Hi," said Molly again.

Homer still couldn't think up anything to say. He combed and smiled, smiled and combed. Then, suddenly, he remembered Godzilla.

"Hi, there," he said, reaching under Molly's desk. "Oh, my, what sharp teeth you've got."

Darryl Pumpwater was sitting in front of Molly. His ears perked up when he heard Homer's words. He thought Homer was talking to Molly.

"And what a cute hairy face you've got too," said Homer. "So fuzzy!"

Darryl leaned back and listened.

"And one more thing," said Homer. He giggled. "I just love your little tail. It's so soft."

Darryl gasped. His face got red.

"Homer, you say such nice things," said Molly. "What a gentleman."

Homer grinned. Talking to Molly was easy!

He put away his comb and took off his jacket.

"Oh, my!" cried Molly. She clapped a hand to her cheek. "Ruth!"

"Huh?" said Homer. "Ruth who?"

"Wowie zowie cowie!" screeched Darryl, turning around. "Number three!"

Homer scratched his head. Suddenly everyone in the class was staring.

"You really are a superstar, aren't you?" said Luis Cruzon. Luis had only one arm. He had been born that way. He came over and felt Homer's sleeve. "This is old. Was he your grandfather or something?"

"My grandfather?" said Homer. "Who?"

Molly punched Homer on the shoulder. "Who? Who! Come on. As if you didn't know."

"But—but . . . I don't!"

"You can't fool me," said Molly. She shook her finger. "Come on. Everyone knows that has to be Babe Ruth's shirt. It's

probably the one he wore in Little League. His number was three, and his name was Ruth." She winked. "But you knew that, right?"

Homer held out the bottom of his shirt and studied it carefully. "Babe Ruth, the greatest baseball player ever," he mumbled. "No wonder Mr. Foster said this was a lucky shirt."

"It's from Mr. Foster?" said Luis.

Homer nodded.

"That makes sense," said Luis. He had short black hair and a chipped front tooth. "Babe Ruth probably worked for the circus after he was done playing baseball. And that's where Mr. Foster met him."

"Of course!" said Darryl.

"So obvious," said Molly.

"Maxie better look out now," said Luis. "Babe Ruth was a homer king, just like you."

"I'm so glad you came to Bayview," said Molly. "You're going to make us famous."

"I am?" said Homer. He winced.

"Isn't this great," said Luis. He shook

his head with wonder. "The new Babe Ruth will be batting for us in the derby." He pretended to swing a bat. "Pow! Won't Maxie be surprised when Homer steps up to the plate!"

Homer looked up from his shirt and forced a smile. Maxie wasn't the only one who was going to be surprised.

CHAPTER 6

Shakes and Shivers

AFTER school Homer headed home. He'd only gone a block when he spotted a big gray dog lying on the sidewalk. Quickly, he crossed the street.

Homer wasn't afraid of the dog. He was afraid of its fur. If the dog got too close, Homer's eyes would water. His nose would run. And before long he'd be quivering and shivering, like a leaf in the wind.

Half a block later he had to cross the

street again. A fat yellow cat was sitting on a fence. Cats made him shake too.

"Hey! Wait up!"

Homer turned around. It was Molly. She was running toward him with one hand out in front.

"Godzilla and I have been following you since school," she said.

Homer looked around for the invisible dog.

"Bad dog! Get down!" yelled Molly, clapping her hands. "I'm sorry. I've told him not to jump on people."

"It's all right," said Homer. He brushed some pretend hairs off his clothes. "I like dogs. I wish I had one of my own."

"I used to have a cat," said Molly. She stared off, remembering. "But now, it's just me and Godzilla."

For a moment Homer thought about telling Molly he had an allergy. But before he could speak Molly said, "Don't you just hate people who don't like dogs and cats?"

Homer gulped back his words.

"Some people don't like dogs because

they bark. Some don't like them because they bite. And some have allergies to them," said Molly. She smiled at Homer. "I'm glad you're the kind of boy who likes dogs."

"Like 'em? I love 'em!" said Homer. "Dogs are the greatest. Especially nice ones like Godzilla."

Suddenly Molly jerked forward. "Hey! Godzilla, come back." She shouted and waved her arms. "Now, just look. He's run off into the park."

Molly and Homer trotted into the park, calling for Godzilla. At the far end of the field was a lone boy and his dog. The boy was hitting baseballs. The dog was fetching them back.

"What a great trick," said Homer.

Molly wasn't paying attention to the boy or his dog. She shaded her eyes with her hand and searched for her make-believe mutt.

"Do you see him?" asked Homer.

"No, but he's here," said Molly. She

lifted the silver whistle from around her neck and held it to her lips. "Watch."

Molly blew on the whistle till her face turned red. Homer couldn't hear anything. But he didn't think he was supposed to. He knew that only dogs could hear a dog whistle.

After a few moments Molly clapped her hands and squealed. "Look! here he comes!"

"He sure is fast," said Homer, pretending.

Molly bent down and swept the invisible pup into her arms.

"I don't know what I'd do without you," she said, spinning about. "You're always there to protect me."

Homer made a muscle. "I'll protect you too," he said softly.

"Isn't he something?" said Molly. She gave Godzilla a squeeze. "Anytime I get in trouble all I need to do is whistle, and he comes running."

"You could whistle for me too," said Homer. He kicked at the ground. "I've seen lots of karate movies. I wouldn't let anyone hurt you."

Molly looked up. "Thank you. That's sweet."

Homer grinned and made another muscle. "Just look. I'm as strong as Superman."

Molly put Godzilla down and felt Homer's little muscle. "Gol-lee! You're right. You got big muscles."

Homer grinned. He kicked out his leg. "See. That's karate."

"Oh, my," said Molly, putting a hand to her mouth.

"No one ever messed with me at my old school," bragged Homer. He patted his chest. "That's the truth."

And it was. Of course, no one had messed with him because no one had paid him any attention. But Homer didn't tell her that.

"Yo, squirt!"

Homer groaned. He didn't even have to turn around to guess who was standing behind him.

It was Maxie Butts. He'd been the boy hitting baseballs to his dog.

"Why, if it isn't the new Babe Ruth," said Maxie. He gave Homer a toothless grin. "Everybody has been talking about you."

Homer shrugged his shoulders. "I'm nothing special," he said.

"That's for sure," said Maxie.

"You'd better not make fun," said Molly. She looked down at Maxie's little tan dog. He was sniffing at Homer's pants. "Homer isn't just a home run hitter. He's a fighter, too, tough as Superman."

"Well . . ." said Homer.

Maxie gave him a poke in the chest. "I still owe you one for that bath you gave me," he said.

"Don't push him too far," said Molly. She poked Maxie in the ribs. "Homer's got muscles like steel."

"I bet!" said Maxie.

"He could flip you over just like that." Molly snapped her fingers. "He knows karate."

42

Maxie snarled and poked Homer's nose. "So you'd like to beat me up, huh?"

Homer took another step back and reached for his comb.

"Make like a dropped melon, Butts. Split!" said Molly.

"Oh, I'm so scared," said Maxie. He laughed.

"You better be scared," said Molly. She grabbed Homer by the arm and yanked him to her side. "Go on. Show Maxie your muscles."

"That's all right," said Homer. He gulped and held up his hands. "I don't want to show off."

"Come on, let's see those puny muscles," said Maxie. He poked around in his pockets. "Wait a minute. Don't make them yet. First I want to get out my magnifying glass."

"Boy, you're asking for it now," said Molly. She tapped Homer on the chest. "Go on. Make a muscle. Show him those cannonballs on your arms."

Homer forced a smile. *Me and my big trap,* he thought.

Maxie growled. He poked Homer in the chest again. Hard.

"I'm waiting for those muscles, tough guy!"

"Well, okay," said Homer. He raised his arm. "I guess I can make . . . SNIFF!" Homer sucked in his nose. It had just started to run.

It wasn't running just a little either. It was like someone had turned on a faucet. "SNIFF! SNIFF! SNNNN-IF!"

"What's wrong? Scared?" said Maxie.

"SNIFF! SNIFF! SNIFF!" answered Homer.

He rubbed his eyes. They were watering too. And just about then his legs started shaking, a lot.

"Homer, are you okay?" asked Molly.

"SNIFF! SNIFF! SNIFF!" replied Homer. He was losing the battle. He couldn't sniff fast enough to keep goop from running out of his nose.

"Eee-yew, gross," said Molly, making a face.

Homer looked down at his shaking legs and saw something that nearly made him faint. It was Maxie's mutt. "Oh, no. A dog," he groaned. "I'm getting an allergy attack!"

He wanted to tell Molly about his allergy. But he didn't dare. If she found out he didn't like dogs, maybe she wouldn't like him anymore.

He wiped his nose with his sleeve.

Shhuuu-lop!

"Homer! Be Superman. Show him those muscles!" said Molly desperately.

The only thing super about Homer was the flood coming out of his nose.

He forced a grin. Then he put a finger alongside his nose and blew.

Blurp! Splash!

"EEEE-YEW!" said Molly and Maxie together.

Homer sniffled one last time then turned and lit out for home.

"Ho-mer!" cried Molly.

"I got to go," said Homer over his shoulder. He'd never been so embarrassed in his life. "Sorry. See you around."

"I knew it all along!" shouted Maxie. "You're a fake!"

"He is not," said Molly. But she didn't sound so sure.

CHAPTER 7

The Meeting

ON WEDNESDAY the Meatballs ate lunch outside on the bleachers. When they were done they all went under the stands and sat cross-legged on the grass.

"Welcome to the Meatballs clubhouse," said their new president, Nicole. She reached up and wiggled her fountain of hair. "Will the meeting please come to order."

Everyone sat up straight.

"Who has old business?" asked Nicole.

"Old business always comes first at a meeting."

"What's old business?" asked Homer.

"It's anything that didn't get decided at our last meeting," explained Nicole.

"But we didn't have a last meeting," said Molly. "This is our first one."

"Good point," said Nicole. "Okay, then. Who has new business?"

No one had any new business either.

"Hmmm," said Nicole. "No old business and no new business. Shall we adjourn?"

"Good idea!" said Darryl. "I move we adjourn."

"Second!" said Molly.

"Third!" said Luis.

"Everyone in favor of adjourning say aye," said Nicole.

"Aye!" shouted the Meatballs.

"The meeting is adjourned," said Nicole. She shook her fountain of hair to make it official. "We'll meet again tomorrow."

"That was fun," said Molly. She was

wearing her special Wednesday bow, a huge plaid one. It sat atop her head like a satellite dish.

"A great Meatball meeting," said Darryl. "I loved it."

"And I love our new clubhouse too," said Nicole. She looked up at the bottoms of the bleacher seats. "It's almost perfect."

"Almost?" said Darryl. As usual his clothes were on inside out. "What else could we possibly want?"

"The Home Run Derby trophy," said Nicole. "Every clubhouse needs a trophy."

"We'll get one. On Friday," said Luis. He tapped Homer on the shoulder. "Right?"

Homer forced a smile. Then he took out his comb and went to work on his hair.

"You're a homer king and a Babe Ruth rolled into one," said Luis. "How can you lose?"

"Let's not get carried away," said Molly. "You know, even Babe Ruth struck out sometimes. So let's not hate Homer if he doesn't win."

Homer stopped combing. "Hate?" he said.

"We'll still let him be in the club, right?" said Molly.

Homer gulped. He had never imagined that his new friends might hate him. Or kick him out of the club. He wished Molly would stop giving everyone ideas.

Molly put her hand alongside her mouth and whispered, "Don't worry. I won't tell them about yesterday in the park. You know, about how scared you were."

"But . . ." said Homer.

"He couldn't lose in a zillion years," said Darryl.

"A zillion years is a long time," said Homer.

"Not for a soo-perstar!" said Nicole. She grinned and wiggled her hair at Homer.

Homer scrunched up his little face. "You know, I've been thinking. Maybe someone else, another Meatball, should enter. Maybe Molly, or Luis."

Everyone laughed. They'd never heard such a silly idea.

Nicole scratched under her arm. She was thinking. Some people thought best while scratching their head. Nicole thought best while tickling her armpit.

"I think the trophy should go in the corner," she said. "Is that all right with everyone?"

"You're the president," said Molly. "But if there's no trophy, let's please not blame Homer."

"Yes, please," mumbled Homer.

"No one is going to be blaming Homer or kicking him out of the club," said Darryl. "Do you know why?"

"Why?" asked Molly.

"Because he's going to win, that's why," said Darryl. He slapped Homer on the back. "You're going to smash a giant homer, right?"

"I'll try," squeaked Homer.

"That's all we ask," said Darryl. "And if you don't win . . . well . . ."

"Well, then, we'll try our best not to be too mean," said Nicole.

Molly made a fist. "That's the Meatball spirit!"

"Thanks," said Homer. "I think."

CHAPTER 8

Practice

HOMER ran all the way home from school to get a bat and a ball. Then he ran to the park to practice hitting homers. There was no time to waste. He had only two days to change from the worst hitter in the school to the best.

The park was empty.

Homer walked to the very center. He looked down at his special T-shirt and tried to pretend that he was Babe Ruth. Then he looked down farther, at his pale green socks. They hung over his black shoes like wilted lettuce.

"Oh, well," he said, with a sigh.

At last he looked around to make sure no one was watching. Then he threw the ball into the air and swung.

"Ooof!"

He didn't hit the ball a mile. He missed it by a mile.

"Maybe I didn't concentrate enough," he said, picking up the ball.

Up went the ball again.

"Ooof!" This time he missed by two miles.

But then . . .

CLINK! on his third try the ball nicked the corner of the bat and dribbled onto the grass.

"Hey! I've almost got it," said Homer. He picked up the ball and threw it super high.

"Whee! Watch out, Maxie," he said. He shut his eyes and yanked back the bat. "I'm going to hit a . . .

"OOOOOF!" Homer swung so hard that

he flew off the ground and spun around like a loose propeller.

"Eeee-yikes!"

THUD! He came down flat on his face.

"Ouch!" he cried.

For a moment little Babe Ruth lay still. Then he began beating on the grass with his fists and kicking the ground with his feet.

"Arrrrrgh!" he growled. "Waaa! Waaa! Waaa! WAAAA!"

Five minutes later he was still beating up on the lawn when someone tapped him on the shoulder.

"What's wrong, Homer? Was the grass mean to you?"

Homer raised up his head. The big blue eyes of Molly James were just inches away. "You must really hate this lawn," she said.

Homer's face got red. There was a lump of mud on his nose. "I—I wasn't fighting the lawn," he stammered. "I was practicing."

"Practicing what? Mowing a lawn with your teeth?" said Molly.

"No. I was working on my hitting," said Homer. He sat up and tried to pull up one of his socks, but it flopped right back over. "I'm trying to get ready for the Home Run Derby."

Molly picked the mud off Homer's nose. "If you don't win, that's okay. Maxie scares me too," she said.

"I'm not afraid of Maxie," said Homer.

"You and I are friends," said Molly, not even listening. "So even though the whole school will be laughing, I'll be standing by your side."

"But, Molly, I'm not afraid of Maxie," said Homer.

Molly closed her eyes. "Friends have to stick together," she said. "Even if their friends are losers and chickens sometimes."

"But, Molly!" said Homer. He cupped a hand to his mouth and shouted. "I told you. I'm not afraid of Maxie Butts!"

Molly opened her eyes. "Huh?"

"I'm not afraid of Maxie," said Homer.

"Don't lie," said Molly. She tapped Homer on the nose. "I saw you shaking the other day."

"I wasn't shaking because I was scared," said Homer. "It was because of Maxie's dog. Animal hair gives me the shivers."

"It does?" said Molly.

Homer raised his hand. "But—but wait. That doesn't mean I don't like Godzilla. He's my kind of dog. I'm not allergic to him."

Molly smiled. "You're allergic, huh? That's amazing!"

Homer tilted his little head. "Amazing? How come?"

"It practically makes us twins," said Molly. "Guess what? I'm allergic too!"

"Really?"

"I can't have any real pets either," said Molly. She lowered her eyes. "I had to give my last cat away. He made me sneeze."

Homer gasped. "I've never known anyone else with a fur allergy."

"You do now," said Molly.

Homer grinned and looked into Molly's big watery blue eyes. He was sorry she had an allergy. But in a way he was glad too. Now they had something to share, something really special; the shakes, the shivers, and the sneezes.

CHAPTER 9

Holding Hands

WHEN Homer got to school on Thursday he discovered a big poster on his classroom door. It said:

HOME OF THE NEXT DERBY CHAMP!

THE NEW BABE RUTH, HOMER KING!!!

"Wow!" said Homer. He flicked some imaginary dust from the collar of his T-shirt and gazed at the poster. He'd never seen his name written so big. Or felt so famous.

Just then Molly came skipping down the hall. She had another giant bow in her hair. Her silver whistle hung on a string around her neck.

Homer stood proudly alongside the poster and cleared his throat.

"A-hem!" he said, pointing at the poster. "Good morning!"

"Hi," said Molly. She stuck out her hand. "Here, hold this."

Homer's eyes got round as pie pans. Did Molly want to hold hands? Right there in the hall? He liked her, sure, but he wasn't about to hold hands. Not right out in public. No way.

"Homer, please, just for a second," said Molly. "While I get a drink of water."

Homer gulped. He looked around nervously. "I don't know," he said.

Molly touched Homer's hand. "Come on. What's the big deal?"

Homer felt like he might faint. He'd never met a girl like Molly.

"Scared?" said Molly. She bent over and tried to look into his eyes.

Homer blushed. "Yeah. A little."

Molly took Homer's hand. "You don't have to be. He won't bite."

"Huh?" Homer looked up. "Who won't bite?"

"Godzilla," said Molly. "I want you to hold his leash while I get a drink of water."

Homer looked down at Molly's hand. "His leash?" He shook his head. Then grinned. "That's it? You only want me to hold his leash?"

"Yes, silly," said Molly. She pressed Godzilla's pretend leash into Homer's hand. "I'll only be a second. Now, don't let him get away."

"I'll take the best care ever," said Homer. He sighed happily with relief. "Don't worry. You can count on me!"

After Molly had skipped to the drinking fountain, Homer bent over and petted the invisible dog. "Nice boy," he said, loud enough for Molly to hear. He wanted to make sure she knew he was doing a good job with her precious puppy. "Don't go anywhere, pal."

As it turned out, Molly wasn't the only one listening to Homer. So were Maxie Butts and Billy Tubbs. The two Jokers were leaning against a nearby locker. Billy was picking at his teeth with a card, the ace of spades. Maxie was fiddling with a plastic flower pinned to his suspenders.

"Cootchy, cootchy coo," went Homer, scratching at the air. "Do you like that?"

Maxie rolled his eyes at Billy.

"Oooh, what a nice cold nose you've got," said Homer. "Cootchy, cootchy, cootchy."

Billy poked Maxie in the ribs. Then spun a finger alongside his head. "I think little Babe Ruth has flipped," he whispered.

Homer looked up. Molly was still getting a drink.

"You're beautiful," said Homer, practically shouting as he petted the air. "Cootchy, cootchy—"

"Coo!" said Maxie, jabbing him from behind.

65

Homer straightened up like a soldier. Red faced, he turned around.

"Boy, you are a silly squirt," said Maxie, hissing out the s's. "Do you enjoy talking to the floor?"

"You should see the nurse," shouted Billy from across the hall. He laughed.

Maxie tapped his head. "If I were you I'd get my noodle examined. Falling in love with a floor is sick."

Homer was too embarrassed to speak. He got out his comb and started re-arranging his hair. He was still combing when Molly returned.

"You should get your friend to the nurse," said Maxie, nodding to Molly. "He's a sick kid."

Molly took the pretend leash from Homer. "What's wrong?" she asked. "Did you get an allergy attack?"

Homer shook his head. "I'm okay," he said.

Maxie grinned and rubbed the plastic flower pinned to his suspenders. "Homer here is a real meatball, that's for sure."

"Make like a truck, Butts. Hit the road," said Molly. "You don't scare us."

"I don't? What about yesterday? In the park," said Maxie. "I sure scared you then."

"I wasn't scared of you," said Homer. He put away his comb. "I was shaking because I have an allergy to dog hair."

"Yeah, sure," said Maxie.

"It's the truth," said Molly. "Your dog gave him an allergy attack. So don't make fun."

Maxie raised an eyebrow. "Are you serious?"

Homer nodded. "Cats make me shake too."

Maxie clucked his tongue. "Gee. That's terrible. Sorry. I didn't know."

"Quit making fun of him! It's not nice to make fun of people's handicaps," said Molly.

Maxie shook his head. "Boy, do I feel rotten." He offered Molly his hand. "I want to apologize. What do you say? Friends?"

Molly took a long look at Maxie's hand.

"Come on. Let's be pals," said Maxie. "Shake."

Molly chewed on her lip and thought. Finally, she stuck out her hand. "Okay, Maxie. Friends."

As Maxie shook, he pulled Molly in close. Then, *SQUIRT!* a stream of water came blasting out of the flower on his suspenders.

KERSPLAT! It hit Molly right smack in the eye.

"Eeee-yikes!" she screamed. Molly was so surprised, she jumped right off the floor. By the time she came down there was a puddle of water under her shoes. She slipped. And started to go down.

"Homer!" she yelled.

Homer wasn't a bit of help. Everything had happened so fast, he'd frozen stiff as a flagpole.

"Eeee-yikes!" screamed Molly. Her arms and legs were churning like eggbeaters. A moment later, KERPLOP!

down she went into the puddle with a splash.

"Molly!" said Homer. He put his hand to his mouth.

Molly glared up at Maxie. Then she did what she always did when she was in trouble. She blew on her little silver whistle.

"Godzilla! Get him!"

Maxie was so busy laughing that he never noticed that he was about to be attacked by a make-believe dog. "Eee-yaw!" he shouted. "Got ya!"

Molly sat on the floor, her teeth clenched. "Homer. Do something!"

Homer's hand was still over his mouth. "What should I do?" he whispered.

Molly rolled her eyes with disgust.

"Here," said Maxie, sticking out his hand, offering to help Molly up. "I'm sorry. I just couldn't resist."

Molly glared at Homer. Then, without thinking, she reached for Maxie's hand. "Thanks. At least there's one gentleman here."

Too late Molly realized her mistake.

Halfway to her feet she found herself staring once again into Maxie's plastic flower.

SQUIRT! Out came the water again.

"Whoa! Yikes!"

Molly went down again. KERPLOP! right into the same little puddle.

At last, Homer sprang into action. He spread his legs and held out his arms. Just like he'd seen someone do in a karate movie.

"Eeee-yaw!" he went, jumping up and down like a puppet on a string. "Better watch out, Butts. I know karate!"

Maxie laughed so hard, he held his sides.

"Ay-yup!" shouted Homer. He kicked out his leg. "I'm serious."

"Seriously silly," said Maxie.

"Oh, yeah?" said Homer. "Watch this!"

Homer leapt into the air and kicked out both feet.

"Whoopsie!" he said, suddenly realizing his mistake.

KER-FLUNK! he crashed onto the floor, bounced once, rolled over, and moaned.

71

"Godzilla!" cried Molly. She jumped up and put her hands to her cheeks. "My baby!"

Maxie hooted and pointed at the karate kid. "See you tomorrow at the derby," he said. Whistling, he disappeared down the hall with Billy Tubbs.

"Homer! How could you?" said Molly.

"Sorry," said Homer. He rubbed his bottom and got to his feet. "I guess I need karate lessons."

"You need more than that," said Molly. "You need to learn how to not be mean."

"Huh?" said Homer. He squinted and rubbed his shoulder.

"You just crashed down on Godzilla's tail."

"I did?" said Homer.

Molly planted herself in the middle of the hall and blew on her whistle. She blew so hard, her face got red. Then purple. But Godzilla didn't come back. Finally, after what seemed like forever, Molly shook her head and moaned. "My poor, poor baby. He's gone. For good."

"For good? Really?" said Homer.

"Well, you don't see him, do you?" said Molly.

"No, but—"

"How could you?" said Molly. "To a precious little dog!"

"I'm sure he'll come back," said Homer.

"He better," said Molly.

But he didn't.

CHAPTER 10

Still Gone

"HOORAY!" shouted Luis the second Homer came walking through the classroom door on Friday. "Three cheers for the next winner of the Home Run Derby!"

"Hooray! Hooray! Hooray!" yelled the class.

"Yip! Yip! Yip!" shouted Nicole. She wagged her fountain of hair with each yip. "Today, at eleven, we get the trophy."

Mr. Foster snatched a banana from the bunch above his desk. He pointed it at Homer. "Don't forget. Besides the trophy you could also earn one of these."

Homer forced a smile. Then he walked to his seat. As he passed down the aisle, everyone slapped him on the back of his Babe Ruth T-shirt.

"It won't even be close," said Luis. "By lunch you'll be the champ."

"No one can beat a Homer King!" said Darryl.

"He's a meatball sooo-perstar!" shouted Nicole, wagging her hair.

Everyone cheered. Everyone but Molly. She was slumped in her seat, blowing on her little silver whistle.

Homer slid into his seat. Then he reached across the aisle and patted Molly's hand. "Still not back?" he asked.

Molly shook her head and stared at her desk.

"Sorry," said Homer.

Molly shrugged her shoulders. There was a huge white bow in her hair, but it had fallen to the side. It looked kind of sad and tired, like Molly.

"It's only been a day," said Homer. "He'll come back."

"I don't think so," said Molly, still not looking up. "You really smashed his tail. I'm sure he thinks we hate him." She sighed, letting the whistle drop from her mouth. "I'm so sad. He was my only friend."

Homer patted Molly's hand. "I'm your friend."

Molly sighed and put her head down on her desk. It didn't look as if anyone was ever going to replace Godzilla. Especially not the boy who'd stomped on her puppy's tail.

CHAPTER 11

The Home Run Derby

MR. FOSTER'S class didn't get a lick of work done all morning. All they could think about was the Home Run Derby. The minutes seemed to crawl by. Time was passing slower than a worm on crutches.

"Two hours to go!" crowed Luis at nine.

"One hour and a half!" yelled Darryl at nine-thirty.

It was like a countdown to New Year's

for everyone in the class but Homer. For him it was a countdown to doom.

Eventually it was ten. Then ten-thirty. Then finally,

BRRRRIIING! Eleven o'clock.

Every door in the school flew open. The students poured into the halls. They raced out the doors and into the sunshine, running and yelling and jumping up and down as if it were the last day of school. Within minutes everyone had gathered on the baseball field.

While Homer combed his hair and looked around for an easy way to escape, Mr. Owens, the gym teacher, announced the derby.

"Attention!" he yelled, cupping his hand alongside his fat red cheeks. "It's time for the Bayview Home Run Derby." He pointed to a trophy on a nearby table. "Whoever hits the farthest ball today will get to keep this in their class or their clubhouse all year."

Luis tapped Homer on the shoulder. "That's going to be us, thanks to you."

"Nobody can beat Babe Ruth," said Nicole. She wiggled her hair. "He's going to make the Meatballs famous."

Homer smiled. Being compared to the great Babe Ruth always made him feel special.

Mr. Foster clamped a hand on Homer's shoulder. "I sure do wish Baby Ruth could be here today. She sure would love to see you wearing her T-shirt. In the history of the circus no one could hit like Baby."

Darryl giggled. "Mr. Foster, you mean Babe Ruth, not Baby Ruth."

Nicole giggled too. So did Homer.

Mr. Foster pulled a banana from his pocket. "We'd give Baby one of these, and pow! she'd smack a ball a mile. The circus fans couldn't get enough of Baby Ruth."

Nicole wiggled her hair for attention. "Don't you mean Babe Ruth? Not Baby Ruth?"

"No, I mean Baby Ruth," said Mr. Foster. "She was a circus monkey. The clowns would pitch her a ball, and wham! she'd hit it into the stands."

Homer looked down at his T-shirt. "You mean all this week I've been wearing a monkey suit?"

"No, only a monkey T-shirt," said Mr. Foster. He waved the banana under Homer's nose. "Remember. Hit a homer and you'll win this tasty treat. Just like Baby Ruth used to."

Homer couldn't get his eyes off his T-shirt. "But—but I thought the Ruth on the back stood for Babe Ruth, the greatest hitter ever."

"Nope. It stands for the greatest monkey ever," said Mr. Foster. "That's even more special."

Homer didn't feel very special. If anything he felt very silly. Maybe even very stupid.

"Does this mean we won't get the trophy?" said Nicole.

"We'll still get it," said Luis. "Don't forget. Our pal's nickname is Homer King."

Homer shook his head. "I've been trying to tell you. Homer King is my real name. Not my nickname."

"Oh," said the Meatballs, nodding. "Hmmmm."

Nicole scratched under her arm and thought. "So let me get this straight. Homer King is your real name. And you're dressed in a monkey outfit?"

Homer nodded.

"Oh," said the Meatballs. "Uh . . . hmmmm."

Homer's hands were suddenly all sweaty. "Does this mean I'm going to get kicked out of the club? Are you going to hate me if I don't win?" he asked nervously.

"Hmmmm," said the Meatballs. They all scratched their heads and thought. All except Nicole. She tweaked her ponytail.

While everyone was scratching and thinking, the first batter stepped to the plate to start off the Home Run Derby.

"Our first batter is Will Hathaway!" announced Mr. Owens. Everyone turned to watch.

Will was wearing bright red pants and a turned-around cap. He stepped to the plate, raised his bat, and watched Mr. Owens's first pitch speed his way.

KRRR-ACKK! He smashed it into the outfield. When it hit, a student marked the spot with a little flag.

After he had hit three times, Susan Price stepped up to bat. Her third hit went farther than Will's, and she took the lead.

Homer shook his head.

"I'm a loser for sure," he said to Molly. He rubbed his sweaty palms on his pants. "I can never hit farther than Susan."

"Or than me," said Maxie, walking up. In his hand he had a little white bag. "Not only am I the greatest hitter at this school, I have all the best equipment." He held up the sack. "Look at this. It's a rosin bag."

"What's a rosin bag?" asked Homer.

"It's got powder in it that dries your hands," explained Maxie. "All the hitters in the big leagues use rosin. It helps them hold on to the bat."

"Make like a drummer, Butts. Beat it!" said Molly.

"Hey, give a guy a chance. I'm only try-

ing to be helpful," said Maxie. He flipped the bag to Homer and Homer caught it. "Your hands look kind of sweaty. Go on. Rub in some rosin. No charge."

Homer shrugged his shoulders and rubbed the bag. Maxie was right. The rosin dried out his damp palms.

"Thanks," he said, returning the bag. "Hey, you're okay."

"Don't thank Maxie," whispered Molly. "I've never seen him do anyone a favor. I bet he's tricking."

"Not this time," said Homer. He held out his hands. "Look. They're dry."

"Eeee-yew!" said Molly, making a face. "What's that yucky stuff on your hands?"

"Huh?" said Homer. He turned his hands to his face. Then gasped.

"Dog hairs!"

Maxie grinned.

Homer couldn't get his eyes off his hairy hands. "Dog hairs! Now I'm going to get sick!"

Maxie slapped a hand to his cheek and looked skyward. "Ooooooh, I bet that bad dog of mine was playing with the bag. Oooooooh, just wait till I get home. That mutt is going to get it!"

"You did it on purpose," said Molly. "You wanted Homer to get sick!"

Molly put her whistle in her mouth and blew. Trouble was on the way. They were going to need help.

Maxie laughed and went off to bat. Mr. Owens had just called his name.

"Wash your hands," said Molly. "Maybe it's not too late."

But it was too late. Homer had already begun shaking, shivering, and sniffling. His nose was running like a cracked fire hydrant. "Rats!" he moaned between snarfs and sniffles. "I've just been knocked from the derby, by a hair."

CHAPTER 12

The Home Run Shivers

HOMER was a mess. His nose was leaking. His eyes were watering. And his body was shaking so bad, it looked as if he might come apart.

Maxie stood at home plate and laughed at Homer. Finally, Mr. Owens put his hands on his hips.

"Are you going to bat or not?" he asked.

Maxie wiped the tears of laughter from his eyes and then raised up his bat. "Ready, Mr. Owens. Pitch it in!"

Mr. Owens pitched. Maxie swung.

WHACK! Maxie sent the ball deep into the outfield.

"Woooo-ee!" he crowed, watching it land. "I'm in the lead!"

The Jokers hooted and yelled. And they cheered again when his next hit went even farther.

"I'm slugging for the stars on the next one!" he said, hissing the *s*'s through the gaps in his teeth. Maxie waved his bat at the crowd. "Get your cameras ready, folks. I'm going for the world record!"

Just as Mr. Owens was winding up for the pitch, Molly pointed to the outfield and screamed.

"Godzilla!" she screeched. She made her hands into binoculars. "My baby! He's coming home!"

"Huh? Godzilla? Coming to home plate? Where? Where?" gasped Maxie. He jerked back his head and searched for a fifty-foot monster with hatched-sized teeth. Too late he realized the pitch was on its way as well. By the time he swung, the ball was nearly past him. Click! the ball hit the edge of the bat and dribbled slowly down the first-base line.

"Hey, no fair!" screamed Maxie. He turned and looked for Molly. "She scared me. That's cheating!"

But Molly never heard his words. She was already out behind second base hugging her make-believe dog.

Homer squinted out of his watery eyes. *Godzilla is back. Now everything will be all right,* he thought.

"Our final batter is Homer King!" announced Mr. Owens, and suddenly Homer realized that everything was not all right at all.

Nicole grabbed her ponytail and waved it at Homer for good luck. "Smack one for the Meatballs," she said.

Mr. Foster held up a banana. "You can do it, Homer. Believe in yourself!"

Homer rubbed his eyes. He could barely see. He couldn't find home plate. Everything looked dark and hazy.

"Homer, you're up," said Mr. Owens.

Maxie laughed. "He's too afraid to bat," he said. "Look at him shaking."

"Homer isn't afraid of anything," said Molly, trotting in from the outfield with Godzilla in her arms. "Can't you see? He's got an allergy."

"I don't care if he's got cooties," said Maxie. "He can't hit. Give me the trophy. The derby is over."

"No, it's not," said Molly. She took Homer by the arm and guided him up to the plate. "You can't stop a Meatball from trying." She glared at Maxie. "Even though you tried."

Homer was shaking like a bean in a blender. His nose was running. So were his eyes.

"Ready?" said Mr. Owens, winding up for the first pitch.

"Rr-r-ready," said Homer. He wasn't even sure where Mr. Owens was.

Mr. Owens pitched. Homer swung, and missed. By about ten miles.

The Jokers howled and slapped each other's hands.

"Are you all right?" asked Mr. Owens, peering in at Homer.

Homer wiped off his nose with his sleeve. He was feeling better, a little. His eyes had cleared and he could at least see.

"I'm all right," he said in his squeaky little voice. "Pitch it again."

Mr. Owens pitched. Homer swung. Click! The ball hit the end of the bat and dribbled onto the grass.

The Jokers howled like hyenas and slapped each other on the back. The Meatballs lowered their heads and shuffled their feet in the dirt.

Nicole looked as if she was going to cry. "I guess that trophy wasn't meant to be in our clubhouse," she said, sniffling.

"Poor Homer," said Molly. She fiddled with her silver whistle. "I feel so bad for him. He's trying so hard."

"Maybe we need to give him a reason to try harder," said Mr. Foster.

Molly looked up. "Like what?"

"Like this," said Mr. Foster, pulling another banana from his pocket. He waved at

91

Homer with the fruit. "Two bananas if you hit a homer!" he yelled. He turned to Molly and winked. "That should do it."

"Maybe," said Molly. But she didn't sound too sure of it.

Now Mr. Owens was winding up for the last pitch.

"It's almost over," said Maxie. He started toward the trophy table. "I'm going to go get my prize."

Mr. Owens pitched.

"Here it comes!" yelled Molly.

Homer raised his bat. Then, SNARF! he cleared his nose and got ready to swing.

Suddenly, a giant allergy shiver went shooting through his body. Homer jerked as if he'd been hit by lightning. The bat snapped forward like a whip. It met the speeding ball over the plate and sent it flying.

KEEEEE-RAAACK!

The sound boomed off the walls of the school.

A cry went up from Darryl Pumpwater's lips. "Wowie cowie kablowie!"

"There it goes!" said Mr. Foster, pointing at the ball with his two bananas.

"I hit it!" shouted Homer.

The ball shot away like a rocket.

It didn't come down for what seemed like forever.

"It's going to beat Maxie!" cried Molly.

"No, it's not," said Maxie. He crossed all his fingers and even two of his toes.

When the ball came down at last it was two feet ahead of Maxie's flag.

"Homer's homer won!" cried Luis. He very nearly leapt out of his shoes. "The Meatballs get the trophy."

"Cheaters," grumbled Maxie, turning away.

"Maybe you shouldn't have given Homer that rosin bag," said Molly. "You ended up giving him the home run shivers."

Maxie grumbled some more then walked off the field, shaking his head. "Cheaters," he mumbled to anyone who would listen.

"The Meatballs are the new champs!"

said Nicole. She couldn't stop wiggling her hair.

Mr. Owens brought Homer the big trophy.

"Here," said Homer, passing it on to Nicole. "You're the head Meatball. You take it."

Nicole sighed. "I know just where this is going to go," she said.

"We'll have the best clubhouse ever," said Molly. She lifted up her big blue eyes and smiled at Homer. "Thanks to you."

Homer blushed and looked down at his floppy socks. "Aw. It was just a lucky hit," he said, shuffling his feet.

Molly hugged Godzilla tight. "This is the happiest day ever. Lucky me. Now I've got two best friends."

"Two?" said Homer, looking up. "Godzilla and who else?"

"You, silly," said Molly. She put a hand to her mouth and giggled.

"Aw," went all the Meatballs.

Mr. Foster presented the two bananas to Homer. "Great hit, kid. I haven't seen a homer like that since my days in the circus."

Everyone clapped. Homer looked down on the bananas as if they were solid gold. Finally he handed one of them to Molly.

"Here," he said. "For my favorite Meatball."

"Thanks," said Molly, blushing.

"Mr. Foster, today you made a monkey out of me," said Homer. He peeled his banana and took a bite. "But you know what? I didn't mind one bit!"

Mr. Foster smiled. He knew his monkeys.

"I thought you'd say that," he said.

FIVE FREAKY SPORTS FACTS

For nearly forty years Babe Ruth held the record for most home runs. He also held the record for most strikeouts.

In 1911 the New York Giants stole a record 347 bases. Toward the end of the season their uniforms got more and more torn by all that sliding. One of the Giants slid into second and his pants ripped right off, leaving him standing on the base in his underwear.

The shortest baseball player to ever play in a major league game was Ernie Gaedel. He was only three feet seven inches tall. He was up to bat only once, on September 2, 1951. He crouched low and the pitcher couldn't pitch a strike. He walked on four straight pitches. His number? 1/8th.

St. Louis pitcher Dizzy Dean was hit in the head by a baseball during a game. He was sent to the hospital for a checkup. When he got back he said, "The doctors X-rayed my head and found nothing."

In 1922 the Chicago Cubs met the St. Louis Cardinals in a doubleheader. Cliff Heathcote played for the Cubs, Max Flack for the Cardinals. Between games St. Louis and Chicago made a trade. In the second game Heathcote and Flack each played for the other team.

Meet the Meatballs again
for their next sporting event in
ALL-STAR MEATBALLS #2

The Terrible Tickler

Will Alvin be able to find a rule against tickling before he wrestles the Terrible Tickler? Meatball Kate tries to show him another way out of his plight by taking him to a professional wrestling match. But the pros don't play by the rules at all, and Alvin has to jump into the ring with the dreaded Vulture and Gentleman James to teach them about fairness. It seems that Kate can't help him after all. Or can she?